D1154208

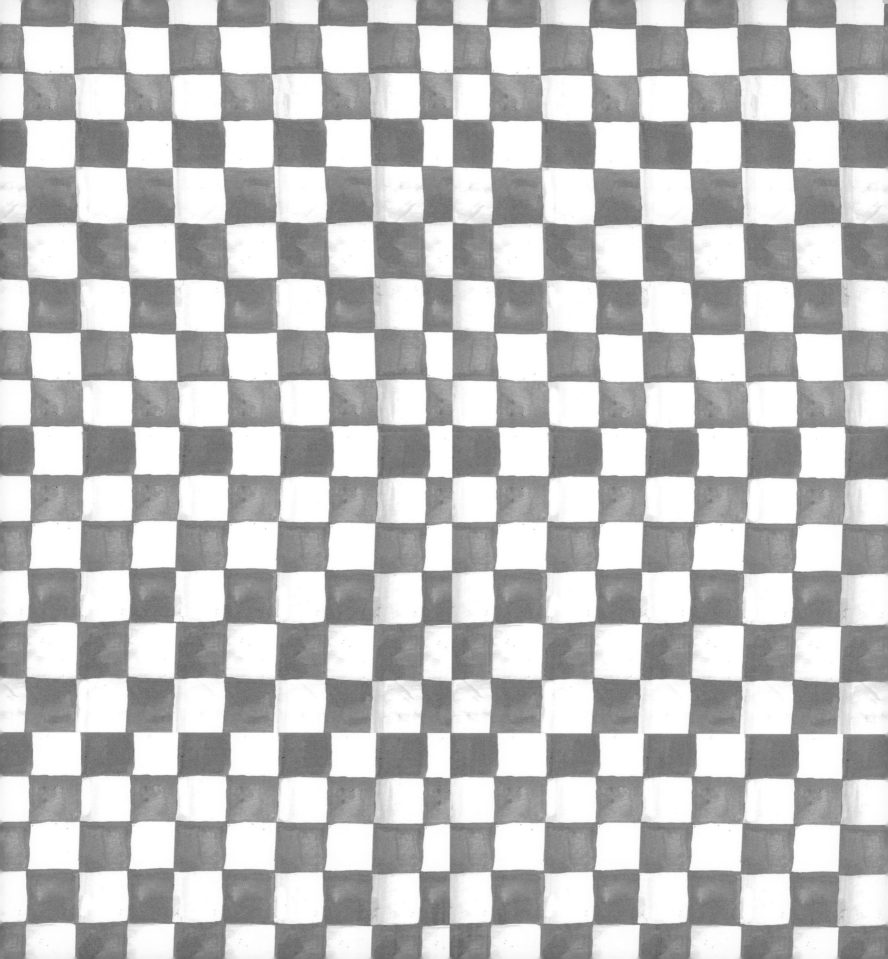

THE PERFECT BIRTHDAY RECIPE

Katy Hudson

SUGAR

CAPSTONE EDITIONS
a capstone imprint

The Perfect Birthday Recipe is published by
Capstone Editions, an imprint of Capstone
1710 Roe Crest Drive
North Mankato, Minnesota 56003
www.capstonepub.com

Library of Congress Cataloging-in-Publication data
is available on the Library of Congress website.

ISBN 978-1-68446-037-3 (hardcover)
ISBN 978-1-68446-039-7 (eBook PDF)

Summary: Summer birthdays can be lonely,
but not when you have great friends like Beaver's!
This year Tortoise, Bird, Rabbit, and Squirrel insist
on baking Beaver's birthday cake, but Beaver
isn't so sure. Will Beaver's picky ways ruin
his birthday and his friendships?

Printed in China.
002493

Designer:
Kay Fraser

For my perfectly
imperfect daughter,
Mabel.—K.H.

Beaver had always liked everything
to be done properly.

Every project he took on
was done **CAREFULLY**.

THOUGHTFULLY.

And as Beaver saw it . . .

PERFECTLY.

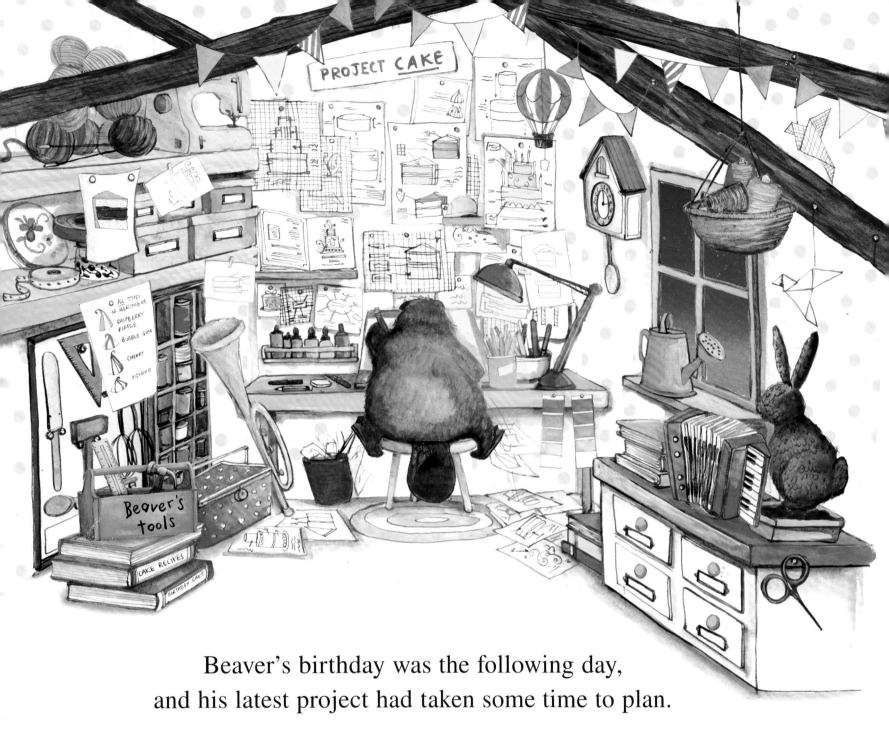

Beaver's birthday was the following day,
and his latest project had taken some time to plan.

It would have a chocolate layer, a carrot layer, a strawberry
layer, another chocolate layer, chocolate swirls, caramel,
frosting, sprinkles, and lots and lots of candles.

It would be the PERFECT birthday cake.

"It's incredible!" said Tortoise, the next day.

"It's ever so big," tweeted Bird. "Will you have enough time to make it all by yourself?"

"Of course not! We'll all help!" offered Rabbit brightly.

"Actually, I have a very specific recipe—" started Beaver.

"BRILLIANT!" interrupted Rabbit. "It will be so much fun to do it together. And for your birthday too!"

But Beaver had planned his cake very carefully. What if his friends didn't read his recipe properly?

As it turns out, Beaver was right to have concerns. On the recipe, "two carrots" looked like "two hundred carrots" to Rabbit.

"Too many carrots!" cried Beaver.

"OOPS!" said Rabbit.

The carrot cake layer
was ruined.

Squirrel could fetch ingredients faster than
Beaver could read them out.

However, she was too fast at getting
them in the mixing bowl . . .

"Is that everything?" Squirrel asked brightly.

"HUMPHHHHGRRRRHUMPH," grumbled Beaver.

SPLAT!

PROJECT CAKE

Ingredients drop off Point ↓ ↙

Borney TRAW JA

CHOCOLA SPREA

GIAN SPR

MABEL'S BAKING POWDER

Self-rising FLOUR

Tortoise worked carefully and slowly.
Maybe a little TOO slowly . . .

"Tortoise! It's dripping everywhere!"
panicked Beaver. "This will never do."

Bird felt it was only right to add
her family's "secret ingredient"
to the chocolate layers.

"**ARGHHHH!** What have you done?" cried Beaver.
"The secret ingredient is marshmallows!"

As the last candle was lit, Beaver's friends happily cheered their work.

"What a perfect cake for you!" clapped Squirrel.

"It took all day, but it was worth it," said Rabbit. **"HAPPY BIRTHDAY!"**

And that was when Beaver **SNAPPED!**

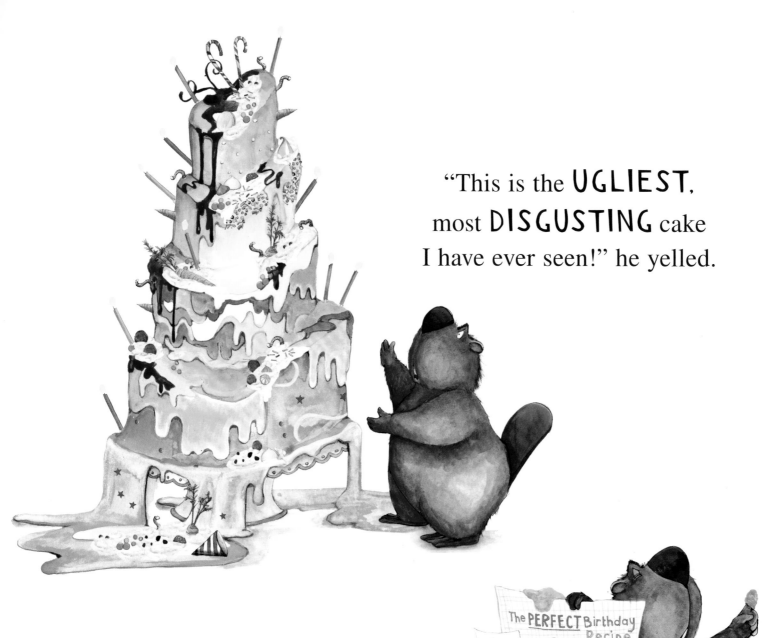

"This is the **UGLIEST**,
most **DISGUSTING** cake
I have ever seen!" he yelled.

"None of you followed
my very clear recipe."

"You used up all my ingredients, and it took you all day.
I will have to start all over again—ALONE!"

While his friends slept,
Beaver worked.
He whisked and he stirred.

He balanced and he spread.

He twirled and he decorated.
Until finally, there it was . . .

. . . his PERFECT birthday cake.
Perfectly baked, perfectly iced,
and perfectly balanced.

And yet it was not perfect at all.
He looked around the empty
picnic blanket and sniffed away a sob.

Then **ANOTHER** and **ANOTHER**
and **ANOTHER** sob—until he couldn't stop.

His poor friends couldn't sleep through all the sobbing.

"I missed my entire birthday trying to make everything perfect, and nothing is perfect at all," Beaver said. "My friends didn't even show up to my party."

"Only because we were sleeping. It is the middle of the night," comforted Rabbit. "Now come on, off to bed."

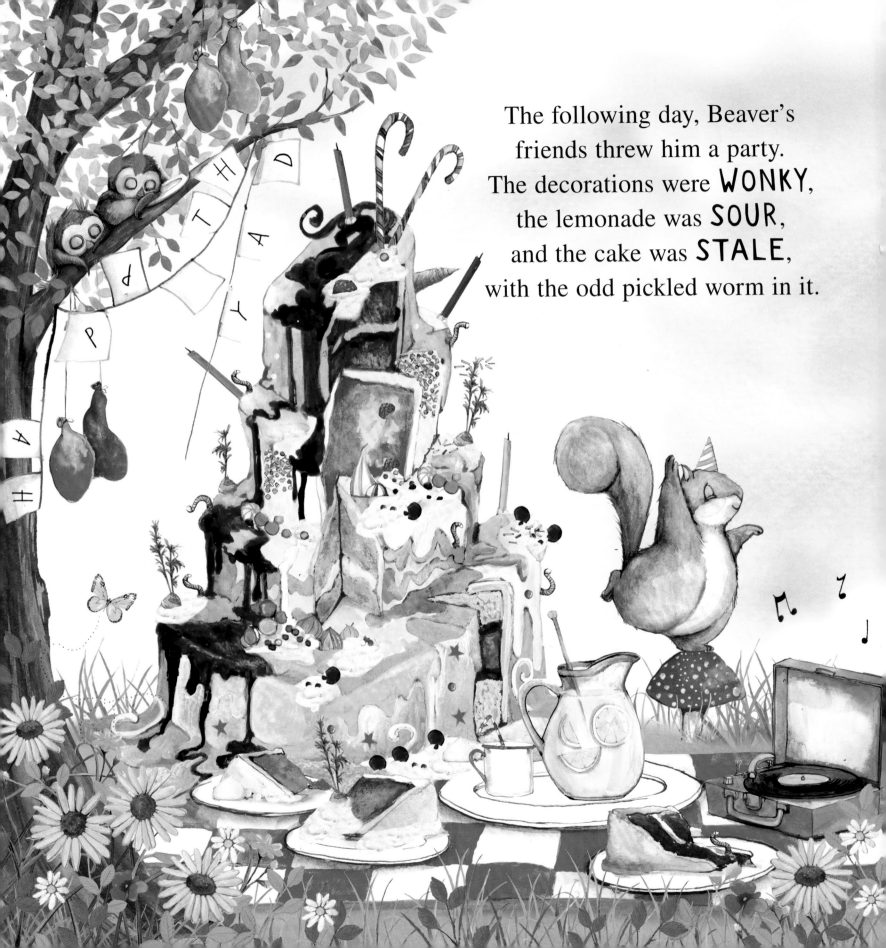

The following day, Beaver's
friends threw him a party.
The decorations were WONKY,
the lemonade was SOUR,
and the cake was STALE,
with the odd pickled worm in it.

It was not at all what Beaver
had planned, but it was the best
birthday he had ever had.
It was, in fact, perfect.

HAPPY BIRTHDAY, BEAVER!

GRAPHIC BIOGRAPHIES

MOTHER JONES
LABOR LEADER

by Connie Colwell Miller

illustrated by Steve Erwin and
Charles Barnett III

Consultant:
Leslie F. Orear
President
Illinois Labor History Society
Chicago, Illinois

Capstone
press

Mankato, Minnesota

Graphic Library is published by Capstone Press,
151 Good Counsel Drive, P.O. Box 669, Mankato, Minnesota 56002.
www.capstonepress.com

Library of Congress Cataloging-in-Publication Data
    Miller, Connie Colwell, 1976–
    Mother Jones : labor leader / by Connie Colwell Miller ; illustrated by Steve Erwin and
Charles Barnett III.
    p. cm. — (Graphic library. Graphic biographies)
    Includes bibliographical references and index.
    Summary: "In graphic novel format, tells the story of Mary "Mother" Jones, a leading labor
union and child labor activist in the late 1800s and early 1900s"—Provided by publisher.
    ISBN-13: 978-0-7368-5487-0 (hardcover)
    ISBN-10: 0-7368-5487-8 (hardcover)
    ISBN-13: 978-0-7368-7535-6 (softcover pbk.)
    ISBN-10: 0-7368-7535-2 (softcover pbk.)
    1. Jones, Mother, 1843?–1930—Juvenile literature. 2. Women labor leaders—United
States—Biography—Juvenile literature. 3. Labor unions—Organizing—United States—
History—Juvenile literature. 4. Child labor—United States—History—Juvenile literature.
5. Women in the labor movement—United States—Biography—Juvenile literature. 6. Graphic
novels. I. Erwin, Steve. II. Barnett, Charles, III. III. Title. IV. Series.
HD8073.J6M55 2007
331.88092—dc22   2006007302

Art Direction and Design
Bob Lentz

Colorist
Melissa Kaercher

Editor
Gillia Olson

Editor's note: Direct quotations from primary sources are indicated by a yellow background.

Direct quotations appear on the following pages:
Pages 7, 8, 11, 16, 26, from *The Autobiography of Mother Jones* by Mary "Mother" Jones
    (Chicago: C. H. Kerr for the Illinois Labor History Society, 1976).
Page 10 from *Mother Jones Speaks: Collected Writings and Speeches*, edited by Philip S. Foner
    (New York: Monad Press, 1983).
Page 17 from the *Philadelphia North American*, July 7, 1903, as quoted in *Mother Jones: The
    Most Dangerous Woman in America* by Elliott J. Gorn (New York: Hill and Wang, 2001).
Page 25: letter from Britt Adams to president Woodrow Wilson, as quoted in *Mother Jones: The
    Most Dangerous Woman in America* by Elliott J. Gorn (New York: Hill and Wang, 2001).

TABLE of CONTENTS

CHAPTER 1
Working Class Struggles 4

CHAPTER 2
Mops and Miners' Wives 10

CHAPTER 3
The Working Children 14

CHAPTER 4
The Most Dangerous Woman in America 20

More about Mother Jones 28

Glossary 30

Internet Sites 30

Read More 31

Bibliography 31

Index 32

Chapter 1
WORKING CLASS STRUGGLES

In the 1840s, young Mary Harris was living with her family in Cork, Ireland. During this time, a disease killed the potato crop, the main Irish food. Irish farmers had no crops to bring in money, or even to eat. People flocked to the cities to find work and food, but there was little of either.

Mary, be thankful we have enough money for flour. That's more than many people have.

Mother, can't we buy a chicken?

But there must be people with extra food. Why can't everyone have some?

At the time, Great Britain controlled Ireland. Most Irish thought of the British as uncaring, foreign intruders. They believed the British response to the potato disease only made the situation worse.

Harris, I miss one rent payment in 20 years and I'm thrown out like a dog!

If you're not making money for 'em, the Brits don't care if you live or die.

If we Irish could all stand together, we could drive out these foreign rats!

Small rebellions took place around the country. But change was too slow to come.

The Harris family decided to try their luck in North America. They moved to Toronto, Canada, in the early 1850s. Life was better, but they were still poor. Everyone helped out.

Good job, Mary. We can use the money from this sewing.

Mary's family did well enough for her to attend school. She even went to a teachers college, an uncommon opportunity for a female Irish immigrant in the 1850s.

5

A teaching job brought Mary to Memphis, Tennessee, where she met, and soon married, George Jones. As they raised their four children in a one-room home, money was always tight.

I hope the leftovers from tonight will last us until the next payday.

George worked as an iron molder in a factory. It was the time of the Industrial Revolution, and George was right in the middle of it.

George, my father had his own shop. He brought home honest money without working in a dungeon 12 hours a day.

Times have changed. All these machines can make parts faster and cheaper than one man in his shop. And, of course, more parts means more money.

Our paychecks don't show it.

What's best for business isn't always best for the workers.

6

Around the country, worker strikes increased. Chicago, as a center of industry, had many protests. For more than a decade, Mary was surrounded by the protests of the working class.

In the mid-1880s, Mary began to attend Knights of Labor meetings.

We work 12-hour days and lose fingers in unsafe machines. All of us are underpaid.

We must demand better wages, safer conditions, and shorter workdays!

We must!

Yes!

In 1894, she marched with Coxey's army. This group of unemployed people went to Washington, D.C., to ask the president for a jobs program.

The farmer down the road was sympathetic, boys. There'll be bread and beans tonight!

Chapter 2
MOPS AND MINERS' WIVES

In the late 1890s, Mary became an organizer for the United Mine Workers union. Coal miners across the country were working, and striking, for better conditions. Mary traveled to wherever she was needed.

I am one of you, and I know what it is to suffer.

But let us think about your lives. You work 12 hours a day, dust choking your lungs.

You'll do this until you die from a cave-in, your lungs have rotted, or your bodies are too abused to work.

In 1899, coal workers in Arnot, Pennsylvania, had been striking for months for better working conditions and pay. When the coal company hired other workers, called scabs, to replace the striking miners, Mother Jones knew she had to help.

Men, you stay home with the kids. The women can deal with the scabs.

Mother Jones organized the miners' wives to keep out the scabs, armed only with mops and brooms. Mother Jones herself couldn't go near the mine or she would be arrested immediately.

No scabs will enter this mine today!

Chapter 3
THE WORKING CHILDREN

In 1903, Mother Jones traveled to the textile mills in Kensington, Pennsylvania, to see the conditions of the workers. Sometimes, she posed as a worker to get inside the mills. Other times, she simply walked in, daring anyone to stop her.

How old are you, young lady?

I'm 10.

How long do you work every day?

I do a 10-hour shift.

And how much are you paid, dear?

$3 a week.

She should be attending school and playing with toys, not working away her youth!

15

Mother Jones wanted to show people the poor treatment of the mill children, so she organized a march.

This city's mansions were built on the broken bones, the quivering hearts, and the drooping heads of these children!

The march continued to New York. At the Coney Island amusement park, Mother Jones took an opportunity to showcase child labor issues. The children got into empty animal cages, while Mother Jones talked to the crowd.

These cages are a symbol. The children are trapped.

Trapped in the textile mills for 10 or 12 hours a day.

They weave the carpets that you walk upon and the clothes you wear.

All they want is good square meals, to go to school, and just a chance to play.

Chapter 4
THE MOST DANGEROUS WOMAN IN AMERICA

Mother Jones continued to travel the country to organize workers.

It's an outrage that the company hires gunmen to enforce its own rules against miners who ask a bit more than slavery!

It's an outrage that a company president should own the coal God put in the earth for all the people.

Miners and company guards did sometimes fight. But often, the only force needed against the unions was an order from a local judge. Judges issued injunctions to stop strikes and union activity, including speeches.

They've come to serve the injunction, boys.

But I wonder why the judge doesn't issue injunctions against the thugs who are beating up our people!

You are illegally interfering with these workers and their jobs. You are under arrest!

I'll be right with you, sheriff.

Goodbye, boys—I'm under arrest. Keep the strike going!

Mother Jones was arrested again in 1913 at the age of 76. She had traveled to Trinidad, Colorado, to help strikers in the coal mines. Upon her arrival, she was arrested and put in a cellar jail cell by the state military, which had been called in to stop violence.

If you promise to leave the strike area, you are free to go.

I won't give up on my boys.

I'm already fighting sewer rats. I can fight the human sewer rats just as well from in here!

Indeed, newspapers wrote how Mother Jones, an old woman, had been placed in jail simply to keep her from speaking to miners. Letters and petitions urged lawmakers, and even President Woodrow Wilson, to let her go.

The old lady is right when she says that the worker has no protection from our government and that the government is run by and for the wealthy

After 26 days, Mother Jones was released.

Releasing me a day before my trial—you knew you had no right to imprison me! And the judge would have said so.

Mother Jones continued to give rousing speeches, into her very old age.

All the average human being asks is something he can call home; a family that is fed and warm; and now and then a little happiness.

MOTHER SAYS

EQUAL JUSTICE

ABOR UNION

Mother Jones was a pioneer in the labor movement. She knew the struggles of the working poor firsthand, and she could speak to workers as one of them. She brought much attention to labor struggles and helped hundreds of thousands of laborers get better treatment.

Mother Jones died in 1930. She asked to be buried alongside coal miners who had been killed during strikes. Her grave is in the Union Miners' Cemetery in Mount Olive, Illinois. Six years after her death, miners erected a monument there in her honor.

SHE GAVE HER LIFE TO THE WORLD OF LABOR, HER BLESSED SOUL TO HEAVEN. GOD'S FINGERS TOUCHED HER—AND NOW SHE SLEEPS.

More about MOTHER JONES

Mother Jones claimed she was born in 1830 in Cork, Ireland. Historians say she was probably born around 1837. No one knows for sure why she claimed to be older than she was.

Mother Jones also claimed May 1 as her birthday. It's unknown when her actual birthday was. May 1 was the date of the mass protest for the 8-hour work day, which she would have seen in Chicago.

Mother Jones claimed that her grandfather was hanged by British troops in Ireland for rebelling against the government. She also claimed that her father left for Canada to avoid arrest due to his rebellious activities. There's no direct evidence of these activities, but Mother Jones surely would have been aware of the problems of the Irish and their feelings toward the British.

Today, a magazine named *Mother Jones* is published. It's a non-profit magazine that aims to be a voice for social justice. It reports on social issues, including the treatment of workers today.

Mother Jones wasn't alive to see Congress pass some of the most important laws in U.S. labor history. In 1932, the Norris-LaGuardia Act barred federal court judges from issuing injunctions against labor unions. In 1938, the Fair Labor Standards Act set a minimum wage and a standard work week. It also outlawed most child labor under age 14. Children ages 14 to 16 could work only outside of school hours.

GLOSSARY

Industrial Revolution (in-DUHSS-tree-uhl rev-uh-LOO-shuhn)— a period from 1790 to 1860 when work began to be done by machines, rather than by hand

scab (SKAB)—someone who takes the job of a union worker who is on strike

strike (STRIKE)—the action of refusing to work because of an argument or a disagreement with an employer over wages or working conditions

union (YOON-yuhn)—an organized group of workers set up to help improve such things as working conditions, wages, and health benefits

yellow fever (YEL-oh FEE-vur)—an illness that can cause high fever, chills, nausea, kidney and liver failure; liver failure causes the skin to become yellow, giving the disease its name.

INTERNET SITES

FactHound offers a safe, fun way to find Internet sites related to this book. All of the sites on FactHound have been researched by our staff.

Here's how:
1. Visit *www.facthound.com*
2. Choose your grade level.
3. Type in this book ID **0736854878** for age-appropriate sites. You may also browse subjects by clicking on letters, or by clicking on pictures and words.
4. Click on the **Fetch It** button.

FactHound will fetch the best sites for you!

READ MORE

Gay, Kathlyn. *Mother Jones.* Greensboro, N.C.: Morgan Reynolds, 2006.

Smith, Nigel. *The Industrial Revolution.* Events & Outcomes. Austin, Texas: Raintree Steck-Vaughn, 2003.

Woog, Adam. *A Sweatshop during the Industrial Revolution.* The Working Life. San Diego: Lucent Books, 2003.

BIBLIOGRAPHY

Atkinson, Linda. *Mother Jones: The Most Dangerous Woman in America.* New York: Crown Publishers, 1978.

Foner, Philip S., editor. *Mother Jones Speaks: Collected Writings and Speeches.* New York: Monad Press, 1983.

Gorn, Elliott J. *Mother Jones: The Most Dangerous Woman in America.* New York: Hill and Wang, 2001.

Jones, Mary Harris. *The Autobiography of Mother Jones.* Chicago: C. H. Kerr for the Illinois Labor History Society, 1976.

INDEX

Canada, 5, 28
Chicago, Illinois, 8–9
child labor, 29
    in coal mines, 18–19
    in factories, 14–15
coal miners, 10–11, 12–13, 18, 20–21, 27
Coxey's army, 9

factories, 6–7, 14–15

Great Chicago Fire, 8

Harris, Ellen (mother), 4
Harris, Richard (father), 5, 28

Industrial Revolution, 6–7
injunctions, 22
Ireland, 4–5, 28

Jones, George (husband), 6–7
Jones, Mary "Mother" (Harris)
    arrests of, 22, 24
    birth of, 28
    children of, 6–7
    death of, 27
    education of, 5
    as seamstress, 5, 8
    on trial, 23

Knights of Labor, 9

labor laws, 19, 29

march of the mill children, 16–17
Memphis, Tennessee, 6–7
Mother Jones magazine, 28

scabs, 12
strikes, 9, 10–11, 19
    Arnot, Pennsylvania, 12–13
    involvement of women in, 12–13
    Trinidad, Colorado, 24
    violence during, 21, 24

unions, 7, 10, 11
    United Mine Workers, 10–11

working conditions, 6–7, 9, 10–11, 12, 14–15, 18, 19